SPORES

A Dark Fairy Tale

E.V. DEAN

For Nuche

FIRST EDITION, MARCH 2025
Copyright © 2025 E.V. Dean

Horror World Books
Los Angeles, California

CHAPTER 1

When I arrived in Baton Rouge, everyone made it a point to tell me that something strange was happening in this small city nestled in the darkest part of the Deep South.

"The sun hasn't come out in months," the janitor at the airport told me. "I've lived here for thirty years and I ain't eva seen nothin' like that."

"It's so dang hot that I just saw a hound dog chasing a rabbit—and they were both walking!" cried the bartender. After I left the airport bar, I noticed that my phone read the temperature at 112 degrees—without the heat of the sun. The air was thick and heavy with a faint metallic aftertaste.

"Animals been goin' missin' out here," explained the waitress at dinner. "I just lost my pit bull last week. He just up and dipped. Never came back. Saw him outside chewin' on one of them yellow things and then he just took off."

"I've never seen a summer this odd," explains the wise and wispy professor. We sit across from each other at a small coffee shop by the university. He clutches his cup of iced coffee with worn and wrinkly hands. His short white hair falls just over the top of his forehead, showing the deep wrinkle in his brow. "I've been teaching here for years and I have never seen a summer without the sun. Crime has been up. It's been so muggy that even now my house is beginning to mold."

That was the main concern of the city of Baton Rouge. The high humidity was causing an unusual amount of fungus to grow. The entire quad of Louisiana State University was speckled with the birth of bright yellow mushrooms. No matter how many times a landscaper plucked the little fuckers, they popped right up in the same spot the next day. In fact, grooming the shrooms appeared to make the problem even worse—they got bigger and bigger, with thick tendrils that dug into the ground. If you picked a small mushroom one afternoon, it was very likely that the next morning you'd find an even bigger one in its place. Maybe you'd even find a dozen new spores.

Nature was not taking their removal kindly.

"I think when they use their equipment to remove them, they are actually spreading the stuff even further," the old man says, letting out a deep sigh. His breath smells like peppermint and coffee with just a hint of last night's whiskey.

Professor Gregory Brighton had begged me to come down to LSU from Columbia to explore what was happening in this strange city.

"Beatrix, I'm so happy you're here." He smiles weakly. His hands tremble as he picks up the napkin from the table and blows his nose into it gently. He sighs deeply and rubs his eyes. They're bloodshot and jaundiced from the increased amount of allergens in the air. "No one wants to really get to the bottom of what's going on. I've called the state, the governor, no one cares. Something bad is happening here. And I think the media is in on it."

"Why do you say that?" I ask.

"Because they keep trying to tell us that those *things* aren't toxic. I don't believe them, I've seen it with my own eyes! I've seen how it changes people the longer they are exposed."

"Well, Dad," I say. "Hopefully I can figure out some way to help."

Like my father, I am a professor but while he studies physics, I study history . . . and the occult. I'm only paid for the former, but the latter is why I am really here. While my father didn't always want to acknowledge my peculiar field of study, he didn't have many options left. His house was slowly becoming consumed by this fungus, and like a stubborn New Yorker, he wasn't planning on leaving Baton Rouge without a solution.

But I am concerned.

How could I not be?

My father lives down here in the strange South all by himself and he refuses to leave. I have to get him out of Louisiana before he gets sick too. My mother passed away a few years ago and I can't bear to see him meet the same fate.

"Hopefully it's nothing," he grumbles. By the furrow of his brow, I can tell he doesn't even believe himself. "Maybe it will be over in a few weeks . . . what do I know?"

My stomach turns. This isn't my father. He's a man of reason and intellect and what is happening here is neither reasonable *nor* intellectual. Something bizarre is happening and the more I talk to people in Baton Rouge, the more irritated I get with their ho-hum complacency for their situation. I grew up in the Northeast and pride myself on being an action taker. I don't wait and sit back and hope for the best. While I like visiting the South, sometimes I can't stand Southern malaise! Where I was raised to tackle problems head-on, I've noticed a tendency here to accept difficulties with a quiet resignation.

My father is getting too complacent.

He lets out a loud sneeze as he shakes. And in that moment, I realize that everyone around me is sneezing or sniffling. Should I wear a mask? Cover my eyes? Take an allergy pill?

How can I keep my father safe if I can't even keep myself safe?

"Beatrix," he says. "I have a student in one of my classes who thinks that he knows where all of this is coming from."

"Really?"

"Yes, his name is Jeremiah. He's a sweet boy from here in town. He told me that there's a spot along the river where all of this is condensed. All of these spores are everywhere—he says it's like a jungle in there of these big heaping fungi. I don't really know what to think. He thinks it's all coming from this spot . . . but I haven't seen it for myself."

"And why is that?"

"Oh, well, you know—it's a bit of a walk off the road in the woods between the road and the river. And it's quite muddy out there given this weather we've been having. You know, my knees don't work so well anymore. I can't go trekking through the swamp like that. Plus, I'm a Yankee. I don't want anything to do with any critters in these woods out here, they are no joke!"

I nod. He has a good point. I'm not too keen on alligators and snakes either. We are New Yorkers to the core. I can handle a big rat and a cockroach, but an alligator is a bit out of the question. Up until my mom passed, I never pictured my father ever living outside the city. Now he was in the Deep South. It was a completely different world.

From what I knew, he was pretty much enjoying his time until things got unsettling.

"I'll connect you with Jeremiah," he says. "He's a sweet boy, a bit odd, but sweet. He can take you to the spot and maybe the two of you can figure out what's causing this mess?"

Do I want to get to the bottom of this strange phenomena? Maybe. Do I want to get my father out of this stinking, rotting, city—absolutely. And I will humor him by any means necessary to make sure I can get him out of Baton Rouge safely.

"Sure," I say. "I'll meet Jeremiah."

CHAPTER 2

I stayed at the university's on-campus hotel, which was a simple but clean little spot by the gymnasium. I wasn't hoping to be here long—maybe a few days max? After all, what can I really do about all of this? Not much.

By trade I am a professor currently working at Robin State College. I am also a world-renowned demonologist, which is why my father called me down to Baton Rouge. It is his view that something strange is happening here that could be *otherworldly*. Demonic even.

But even if that is true, what can I do about it? Not much.

It's the most frustrating thing about my profession. I can diagnose a problem, but I can't provide a solution. Not to mention, no one would really believe me if I said, "Hey, Baton Rouge, there's a pesky demon in your midst causing your city to break out in a barrage of fungus!"

And if this was caused by a demon—it's not like I am an exorcist or anything! I'm not an exorcist. I'm not a priest. I am just your regular old academic with a highly unusual specialty.

Most of the exorcists I know are quite useless in extreme situations. In my years in Paris, Rome, Guangzhou, Milan—having desperate people ask me to help diagnose the otherworldly things that are happening to them—a diagnosis is really all I could give. Even the best exorcist leads to few good changes in a possessed person's situation. Oftentimes, that person is tormented for life.

Usually, the best thing that someone like myself can do is just let these things run their course and give folks the peace of mind that they aren't *crazy*. That they are possessed and experiencing something otherworldly. Usually it gives them a little peace of mind, but that's about it.

I am a doctor who can't treat my patients. And it's fucking exhausting.

It's why I didn't really want to come down here in the first place. The only thing that brings me down to Baton Rouge is curiosity and a small hope that I can coax my father to leave before things get worse.

When I arrive at my hotel that afternoon, I am greeted by a young student at the front desk who gives me a woozy smile. Her eyes are bloodshot and have just a glimmer of jaundice. She has long blond hair and looks like she could be a sorority girl—maybe she is—but the poor girl looks so terribly ill.

"Hello, ma'am," she says slowly. "Checking in?" Her Southern drawl is somehow slower as if she's stopping to consider every next word.

"Yes," I say nodding. I peer around the lobby, which is otherwise empty. No one is quite interested in staying in Baton Rouge at this time. "Do the rooms have filtered air?"

The young woman nods. "You worried about the mushrooms?"

I nod.

"Well, you know, you get used to it. I don't even notice it anymore," she says as she itches her blotchy arms. She rolls up her sleeves to reveal a ripping red rash. "I'm allergic to it, so I have a bit of a worse reaction. But trust me. After a few days here, you won't even notice it."

When I walk into my room, I am greeted by a gust of air-conditioning. The room is freezing and quite quickly I see why. I walk up to the window that should have a great view of the Peter Mavarich Assembly Center, but it's partially blocked by stubborn yellow spores sticking to the windows. In the crevices of the window a little yellow gooey foam looks like it's about to seep in at any moment.

"I can't stay here," I say to myself, laughing. But I know that my father's home is only worse and he simply won't leave it. He's stubborn. When he moved to Louisiana he bought a beautiful little house on University Lake, but even he admits that the fungus has taken over. It's in his windows, in the crevices of his door; even leaving a loaf of bread out for more than a day or two will produce a little colony of yellow spores.

I walk over to the long, full-length mirror that hangs by the bathroom. I look tired. My pale skin, which is usually quite flawless, already has a few blotches on my rosy cheeks. My green eyes are already looking a bit pinkish. Are they itchy? Or am I paranoid? *I just feel itchy.* My bones feel like they are going to crawl out of my skin. And it's hot. It's so very hot. I pull back my long black hair into a messy bun on my head and walk over to the bed.

My mother always taught me to look for bed bugs when I stay in a hotel. I peel back the white comforter and it's damp. Everything is damp. The comforter, the sheets, the mattress, it's all just a bit wet and has just a hint of mildew.

I want to check into another hotel.

But what will be different across town? Probably nothing much. How can anything really dry in such rampant humidity?

Plus I'm exhausted.

And I'm starting to get a bit of a headache.

Anxiously, I lay down on the bed and take a deep breath and force myself to close my eyes. My skin is crawling, my eyes are itchy, and I am trying my best to convince myself that I am just being paranoid.

But what if I am already being affected by the spores?

It would make sense. They are *everywhere*.

I take a deep breath and open my eyes and stare up at the white popcorn ceiling. In the far corner of the ceiling toward the door I see one: a small yellow cap of a tiny mushroom just peeking out of one of the ceiling tiles. It's about the size of a walnut.

Part of me wants to pluck it but my father's warning stops me. I don't want it to spread. I don't want to touch them. I don't want to get infected.

I try to close my eyes to sleep but I can't help but feel that the small little spore in the corner of the room is watching my every move. Should I change rooms? I want to . . . but I'm too exhausted.

There's not much I can do anyway.

They are everywhere. They are abundant.

There is only one of me and millions of them.

CHAPTER 3

When I wake up the next morning my throat is full of a thick mucus gunk. I can barely open my eyes. They're swollen and watery—like I have a thin layer of conjunctivitis that is blurring my vision. I roll over in bed and see the glass of water that I set out the night before. There's a thin yellow film that has risen to the surface. It makes me wonder if I should be drinking the water here at all.

My father set up a time for me to meet with his student Jeremiah for breakfast at the hotel, so I do my best to pull myself out of bed. I take a quick hot shower, doing my best to wash away the feeling that I have that I slept somewhere contaminated and unclean.

I throw on a light sundress. I'm not much of a dress person but when it's over one hundred degrees and sluggishly humid, anything light will do. When I open the door to the hallway, I am met with a gush of warm air that is so hot and heavy I want to retreat back into my room and curl up in the bed. But I can't. I have to push through.

I have to get to the bottom of this.

I have to get my father out of here.

The longer I stay in Baton Rouge the more likely it is that I could become affected by the spores. I don't have to necessarily solve what's happening here, but I do need to put in some effort to show my father that I at least tried to solve this mystery. It's the only way I am going to be able to convince him to leave. If there is some fantastic creature behind all of this, it is much more motivating for my father to leave. But who knows! It could be a biohazard or an invasive species. Not everything wrong in the world has to do with magic.

One time, I had a client fly me all the way out to Kauai to investigate weird symbols that were being drawn in the sand outside of a very popular resort. It turned out to be a few bored local kids. Another client in Greece thought that his house was haunted by an old ancient ghost due to the strange noises happening late at night. It turned out he had a severe problem with his plumbing. You see, not everything strange has to do with the paranormal. And I was praying that this very strange situation in Baton Rouge would have a very normal solution.

When my father told me Jeremiah was "sweet but strange"—he was not lying. Jeremiah sits across from me in the atrium of the hotel, which has been fashioned into a little breakfast spot. The glass windows that cover the ceiling and the walls around us have a faint tinge of yellow.

Jeremiah sits across from me as he enthusiastically sips on his orange juice as if it's the last glass in the world. Jeremiah is older than your average college student—maybe twenty-four or twenty-five. He tells me that he just transferred to LSU from Baton Rouge Community College this year and he is studying engineering.

Like everyone else who has stayed too long in Baton Rouge, his eyes are watery and bloodshot. His brown curly hair falls right above his eyebrows and his ringlets shake as he talks.

He devours his breakfast like it's his last supper, plowing through the eggs, bacon, and sausage on his plate. I can't even imagine eating anything here given the invasive fungus that surrounds us, but Jeremiah seems to have no problem.

"There was one coming out of its brain," Jeremiah said enthusiastically as he took a bite of his sausage. "Like— imagine a dead rabbit with its cranium cracked and little yellow shrooms just sprouting out."

My stomach turns.

I found myself wanting to know if the spores caused the rabbit to die or if it was already dead before the spores got there.

"Why were you guys out there in the first place?" I ask as I swirl a spoon around in my coffee. I haven't had a sip yet. I'm too paranoid that it's infected.

"Well, ma'am, I don't know," Jeremiah says as he takes another hearty bite of his meal. "Ain't much to do in Baton Rouge. So we thought we would follow the mushrooms."

"What do you mean by that?"

"Well yeah, when me and my buddy was fishing by the river, we noticed where them mushrooms started getting closer together. It was like a line that just kept getting thicker and thicker. We followed it a little bit but got tired out. So we came back the next day and followed it all the way into them woods, and that's when we found it."

"Found what?" I ask.

"The center of it all!" he says as his eyes widen. "Tried to get the police out there. They weren't interested. Asked me if I was on drugs."

"Are you?"

Jeremiah shrugs. "I mean—occasional recreational use is no way to discredit what I saw out there. Think of the biggest mushroom you done saw in your life. Must have weighed five hundred pounds. Bigger than a forklift."

"What else did you see?"

"All them animals around it are dead. Eaten up by them mushrooms. Smells like rotten eggs and blood. Like metal almost. Me and my buddy, we had to get out of there fast as we could—it was making us sick to our stomachs. Started messing with our heads even. That smell was so strong you could taste it on your tongue."

I nod and lean into the table, lowering my voice to a whisper. "You remember where it is? Can you take me back there."

Jeremiah nods enthusiastically. "Ma'am, if I may, I have to take you back there. Your daddy done told me that you can stop all this. That you can help us fix our city."

"Well—that's not exactly right I—"

For the first time in our conversation, Jeremiah puts down his fork and places his hands on the table. "It's important.

Dr. Brighton, our city needs your help. Nobody's listening to us. Nobody cares. It's like everybody's just OK breathing in all this mess. They're acting like it's just some bad weather and not something that's gonna make us sick. I know it sounds crazy but there's something in them woods causing this. In the swamp. I just know it. And if these demons and creatures are real like your daddy says they are—"

My heart flutters for a moment. "He told you they were real?" My father has always been very hesitant to accept my expertise. I've never been sure if it's because he really doesn't believe in the paranormal or if it's because he doesn't want to believe in anything otherworldly.

"Yes," Jeremiah says with enthusiasm. "That's why he brought you here, isn't it? To help us?"

CHAPTER 4

The only person I was in Baton Rouge to help was my father. I'm not a superhero. I can't save the world. But maybe I can help my dad from becoming a victim of the spores like those poor animals that Jeremiah described.

When my father called me a few weeks ago talking about the mushrooms, I didn't think much of it at first. Baton Rouge is always a humid place in the summer. The air has always been thick and soupy. It's really no place for anyone at this time of year, unless you're comfortable being uncomfortable. There's a reason people call it the armpit of Louisiana: hot, humid, and unbearable.

But as the days went by, the spores began to spread like a virus. What my father originally described as an influx of wild mushrooms quickly spread across the rolling green grass at the university. And then it got worse.

"The sun has disappeared, Bea," my father told me one morning. I was sitting on my porch in Robin, New Hampshire, enjoying a nice cup of coffee in the warm summer morning.

"What do you mean—the sun is gone?" I asked.

"It's the strangest thing, Bea," my father said as his voice shook. "We haven't seen the sun in days. It just disappeared behind these big black yellowish clouds. And it doesn't rain!

They just hang over the city like a . . . thick blanket of rotten wool. And the smell—God, the smell. Like someone lit a thousand matches and mixed it with spoiled milk."

Just a few days after he called me about the sun, he asked that I come down to Baton Rouge. My father almost never calls me at night. Usually it's a call once or twice every few months just to say hello and to check in. But just a few days ago on one summer night, he called me at almost eleven o'clock. I was sitting in my living room sipping a glass of wine and reading a book when my phone rang.

I got up and walked over to my rotary phone that hung on the wall in the kitchen and picked it up quickly.

"Hello?"

"Bea, it's your father." His voice was shaking again.

"Are you OK?"

"Beatrix, I think something is very wrong." Even though I couldn't see my father, I could tell that he wasn't feeling well. His voice was weak and foggy and it sounded like he had the flu. "It's getting worse. The mushrooms. They're in my house."

My stomach turned. "What do you mean, they're in your house?"

"I went down to the basement to look in my storage and they are everywhere!"

"Everywhere?"

"The whole floor is covered in them. They consumed everything—my books, my clothes, they're covered in the little buggers and every time I try to pluck them off, they grow back the next day."

"Dad, you have to get out of Baton Rouge until this is gone," I said. "I'll buy you a ticket so you can come stay with me in New Hampshire. I have a huge house with plenty of room."

"I can't leave the house," my father said. "What if something happens!"

"Your health is what is most important," I said. "Forget about the house. You have insurance, right?"

"Right."

"So leave! Who knows how this is affecting your health."

I'm met with silence on the other line.

"Dad?"

"Beatrix—can I ask you a question?"

"Sure but, Dad, I really want you to come home. I—"

"What if something unnatural is causing this?" His voice hangs on each word like he can't even believe he's saying it himself.

"What do you mean?" I asked.

"I would feel more comfortable if you came down and took a look at this, Beatrix. What's happening here is not natural. This isn't normal. This is an infection. The city is sick. Something has to be causing this."

My eyes widened. "Are you saying—"

"I just think you should come down here. Something bad is happening, Bea. Maybe something evil."

CHAPTER 5

When I walk out of the hotel and into the large parking lot, I see the cars covered in a yellow dusty film. It looks like someone sprayed pollen all over the cars. Not one car is untouched. Like yesterday, the sun is hidden behind big dark gray clouds and the air is thick. Walking outside is like walking into a heated oven.

I walk over to my rental car, which is a simple Ford Taurus. Even the formerly shiny metal handle is covered in the yellow dust. Trying my best to avoid the residue, I gingerly open the door using just the tips of my fingers and slide into the driver's seat.

My head pounds.

I need coffee.

I didn't want to drink the coffee in the hotel because I don't trust the water. Maybe the coffee shop up the street is better.

Inside the car provides a bit of relief from the spores and I can breathe a bit easier. I turn on the windshield wipers and it forces away the yellow slime, leaving a streaky sludge across my windshield. I use the windshield cleaner, but it almost makes the problem worse—smearing the sulfur-colored powder across the glass.

It's not perfect but it will have to do. I have plans.

It's time to go to the other side of the lake to see my father and hopefully convince him to leave Baton Rouge. I don't want to run through the woods with one of his students. I don't want to sit in a mushroom-filled hotel. I want to get him out of this town.

My father lives on the other side of University Lake, and on my way to his house is the small coffee shop where we met yesterday afternoon. It's a busy little beanery usually swarming with students and professors.

When I walk in I am shocked to see it's eerily empty. While yesterday the place was buzzing with activity, there are no customers here now. At the counter is an older man in his fifties with bloodshot, watery eyes. He's moving around frantically as he dumps things into a giant trash can behind the counter.

He jumps when he sees me walk through the door.

"Ma'am, we are closed."

"Oh, sorry," I say. I look behind me at the sign on the door that says OPEN.

The old man lets a tear fall from his eye.

I want to leave, but something tells me to stay. "Are you OK?" I ask him.

He shakes his head. "No. Not even a little bit."

"Can I help you?"

"Unless you have the money to replace my inventory, no, ma'am. Twelve hundred dollars in inventory gone overnight," he says. "Woke up this morning to spoiled beans. Those yellow fuckers were sprouting right out of the bag. Our pastries too— gone. Flour—gone. It's all gone. I have nothing left."

My father lived just around the lake from the coffee shop in a small house right off the water. The day he bought it, he called me to celebrate what a bargain he got. According to him, it was a quaint little yellow ranch right by the water. I had never been there, of course. Nothing bad—I've just been a bit tied up since he moved down South. But he talked about the house in such eloquent detail that I felt like I had been there some time in my dreams.

If there was one thing my father loved the most about that house, it was the big wraparound porch that covered the ranch from the front all the way to the back. When I was growing up in the Hudson Valley, our old farmhouse had a porch and my father and I would sit outside every day in the spring, summer, and fall as we sipped on tea and read our books. At my home in New Hampshire, I have a porch now too because of my father. I can't imagine living without one. Even when we lived in the city, we had the perfect little balcony that looked right out at the Hudson.

I was excited to see my father's home for the first time, but I was also nervous. He warned me that the spores were slowly beginning to encroach on his home—but when I turned the corner into his driveway, I was unprepared for what I saw.

Where I had imagined green luscious grass leading up to my father's little ranch there was a sea of yellow sprouted mushrooms just dancing in the daytime. As I pulled into the driveway it almost looked like steam was rising off of them in the humid Baton Rouge heat. And then there was the porch. The white gorgeous wraparound that I had imagined was equally infected. Little clusters of mushrooms sprouted off of the floor and the railings, creating clusters of varying sizes. It looked like my father's house was covered in warts.

And whereas I hoped that my father would be sitting inside with the air filter on, he was doing the exact opposite. He sat on the porch in his rocking chair, reading the newspaper and sipping on his coffee. When I pulled into the driveway, he looked up, put down his copy of *The Advocate* and stood up slowly. His eyes were stained with red and he sneezed as he began to walk off the porch toward me.

I put the car in park and eased out of the car. "Dad, go inside! It's not safe out here."

As he walked toward me he waved me off. "Ah, Bea, it's not that bad. What am I supposed to do? Sit inside all day?"

"Yes!" I say as I walk toward him. He already looks worse than yesterday. Somehow frailer and more pale. The bags under his eyes have deepened as he looks up at me. My father used to be taller than me, but as he has aged he's gotten smaller and smaller. Now he looks up at me with his green, bloodshot eyes and his glasses just perched upon his nose.

24

"Well, do you want to see the inside of the house?" he says letting out a small smile.

My stomach turns. By the looks of the outside, I worry that the inside won't be much better. What my father has called his prized possession is covered in a series of boils and warts that must be growing bigger and bigger every day.

"The inside of the house is much nicer than the outside," he says with a loose smile. He grabs my hand and pulls me toward him. "Come on inside, Bea."

When he drags me onto the porch I can't help but look at the mushrooms that are clinging to the railing, the floor—they are everywhere! My father's house is infested with these little yellow buggers.

"Dad," I say as he goes to pull me into the house. "This isn't OK, you can't live like this with all of these spores everywhere. It's going to make you sick."

He waves me off. "Eh, I'm used to it." He takes my hand as he opens the door with the other and leads me into the house. I am met with a burst of a suffocating mold smell. I catch it in my throat like a dry, scratchy sting. I feel my breath slipping away as he pulls me into the house.

And then I see them.

Everywhere.

He takes me into the foyer of the house, which is filled wall-to-wall with the sprouted little devils on each wall. Some are in clusters as big as a frying pan while others are placed more sporadically throughout the white walls of the entrance.

I grab my father's hand tighter.

"Dad, you can't live like this," I say as I look around at the mushrooms that have invaded my father's home.

"Like what?" he says with indignation.

I let go of his hand and gesture at the big white wall covered in spores. "Do you see this?" I ask. "It's making you sick, Dad."

He shrugs. He's wearing an old LSU Tigers football T-shirt that is too big for him. It fits too big on his shoulders as he rocks back and forth on his heels. "Beatrix, if I could be honest, I didn't even notice the mushrooms until you pointed them out just now."

My heart drops. Is my father delusional? Have they gotten to his brain? I walk up to one of the big clusters of mushrooms and grab the fattest and thickest one in my hand. I squeeze it and watch as the yellow powder falls off of the cap causing a mustard-color cloud of dust.

"Don't do that!" my father yells. "You're going to hurt them. They are part of the house. They didn't do anything wrong!" His eyes are wide as he walks up to me, crazed and agitated. He takes his hand and grabs my wrist that is still holding on to the mushroom cap.

"Stop that, Beatrix! You're hurting it!"

His words cause the hairs on the back of my neck to raise. This isn't normal. This isn't OK. Something is happening here that's poisoning my father's brain. He's rational to a fault. He'd never allow his house to be invaded by anything! Especially not mushrooms.

I let go of the mushroom and walk over to my father and put my hands on his shoulders. "Dad, I am really, really worried about you," I say. "I think you should get out of here. We will pack up your stuff and you can come with me to New Hampshire—"

My father's face contorts. His eyebrows furl and his lips turn into the same kind of expression you make when you eat something sour. "I would never leave my home!" he says as his face turns red. "This is my house. I can't leave it."

I shake my head and let go of his shoulders, walking further into his house of horrors. It only gets worse. When I walk into his kitchen, a big loaf of bread on the counter has spores sprouting all over it. The fridge has a rim of yellow just peeking out from the insides of the refrigerator. Even the white tiles on the floor have little sprouts of yellow growing out in the middle of the grout.

My father follows me into the kitchen.

"Can I get you something to drink?" he asks.

I shake my head. I don't want anything from this place at all.

When he opens the fridge, my breath leaves my chest. He opens his fridge to reveal an entire chest full of fungi. There are fungi in the corners of the fridge, on every side, and spouting off of all the food inside the refrigerator.

With unyielding confidence my father reaches into the fridge to pull out a carton of milk. He grabs a glass from the cupboard and pours the milk into the glass. It's not milk, though. It's a thick, yellow, sprouty concoction that looks more like bile than milk.

"Do you want one?" he says as he raises his glass.

As I look at my father holding the putrid glass of bile I can't help but cringe. I have to help him. I have to get him out of this terrible situation. He needs to leave Baton Rouge.

"Dad, we need to go," I say as my voice shakes. "The spores are getting to you."

He smiles and takes a long sip of the yellow sludge. "It's not too bad once you get used to it. Sure, life gets a little fuzzy. A bit slower. But maybe it's a good thing! Why do we need to rush?"

As I watch him guzzle this poison, I realize, I have to get to the bottom of this. It's the only way to get my father out of this hell.

CHAPTER 6

After visiting my father, I have only one objective: to get him out of Baton Rouge as quickly as I can. And if I have to discover what is *really* happening in this town, then so be it. I will figure it out. Maybe it is a demon! Maybe it's a biohazard. Whatever it is, maybe a dose of reality will get my father to make the right choice. The only choice.

I scurry back to the hotel as quickly as I can and call Jeremiah.

Jeremiah agrees to meet me that afternoon at my hotel to take me out to the spot where he thinks the mushrooms originated. He says that if we get there around sunset, we are less likely to feel the oppressive summer heat and that hopefully the gaseous fungi won't be as bad.

As I stand in my hotel room, looking at that pesky yellow spore on the ceiling, I can't believe I am about to do this. His stories of rotting rabbits with growths splitting out of their brains flood my thoughts.

What if I get sick?

What if I get stuck out there in the Louisiana bayou with all of these yellow little creatures growing and spewing their mustard-color dust in the air?

What if I don't make it back to get my father out of this hell?

With every minute I stay in this city, I feel my body getting weaker and weaker. My nasal passages are getting more and more congested and my chest is tightening like there's an inflated balloon in my lungs getting bigger, making it harder to breathe.

I lay down on the moist hotel bed and look up at the little spore on the ceiling. You know, they say that fungus can think. That it can learn and make decisions. They say that mushrooms can remember information about their environment and use it to guide their growth.

What has it learned about us?

Is it watching me?

Is it thinking about me?

When I come back tonight will the little yellow spore have doubled or tripled?

My mind spirals as I stare up at the ceiling. My head feels heavy and I drift off to sleep.

When I wake up, it's late. I look at the alarm clock next to the bed and remember that Jeremiah will be here any minute. I quickly get up and throw on an outfit a bit more practical—leggings, a long-sleeved shirt, and some boots. I've never been in the wilderness out here before. All I know is what I've seen on television—swamps, snakes, rats, and alligators.

I'm a city girl.

I'm not meant for this.

But by the same token, I can't have my father stay here one minute longer.

I grab a protein bar from my purse and scarf it down quickly. No matter what I eat here, I feel like it's infected. But my stomach is groaning and moaning—I have to eat a real meal soon, but I don't even know if I can force myself to. Even the air tastes rotten.

When I get outside it feels like it's getting darker. I am still sweating as I walk outside the hotel and into the parking lot. Despite this, I pull the collar of my sweatshirt up over my nose.

Fluorescent streetlights hang above the pavement as big bugs swarm the lights. Typically the lights wouldn't be on this early, but since the sun left, it's been getting pretty dark in the late afternoons. Now that it's even more humid in Baton Rouge it feels like even the bugs have gotten bigger since I arrived. In the Northeast, we don't have bugs this big. But today, the bugs that dance around the streetlights look like the size of the ones I saw in Southern Brazil. I want nothing to do with them.

Jeremiah is standing outside his car, a rusty pickup truck, while he holds two big bags that are from the hardware store. He smiles as I walk up to him. He looks excited to see me. His yellowy, toothy grin shows from ear to ear.

As I walk toward him, I can't believe I am doing this. I can't believe I am walking out into the dark, Southern swamp with a complete stranger. In my time studying the occult, I've

31

been to some strange places and seen some pretty frightening things. I've seen demons in Rome, vampires in Sydney, ghosts in Poughkeepsie—but I've never gone into a swamp at night where there are more normal dangers of this world. Alligators, snakes, wild boar—I am much more afraid of the normal things that could be found in the bayou.

"Evening, Ms. Brighton," Jeremiah says as he puts down his bags and waves. His long fingers move back and forth so quickly that they look like a blur.

The clouds still cover the sky, trapping in the heat and the gaseous vapor of the mushrooms. As I walk up to Jeremiah's truck I notice that little yellow spores are growing out of the truck's rusty crevices.

"I got us some gear!" Jeremiah says smiling. He reaches into his bag and pulls out a mask with two big black vents on each side.

Jeremiah tosses the mask to me and I catch it by the stretchy elastic band.

"Do you think we will really need to wear these?" I ask. I've never worn a mask like this before.

Jeremiah nods. "Last time I went out there I'm surprised I didn't come back lookin' like I'd been dragged through the swamp backward."

I look down at the mask—it looks so foreign. Like something you'd find in a bomb shelter. But if it prevents me from breathing in any more of this rot—I am all for it.

Jeremiah reaches down into the bag and pulls out a pair of long black rubber gloves. "Got these too. Not smart touchin' all these spores. Way folks round here acting, wouldn't surprise me if they were poison."

"And how do you think they're acting?" I ask as I look up from the mask.

"Well shoot. From what I can tell, folks round here are actin' like a raccoon in a washing machine—ain't never seen nothin' like it."

CHAPTER 7

Jeremiah insists that we take his truck out to the swamp. I feel quite a bit less safe in his vehicle than I would in my rental, but he has a good point.

"Once we get off the road, your little car isn't going to be able to handle the roads out there. It's thick and full of mud. You'll surely get it stuck," he says. "We can take my truck. It will get us to where we need to go, no problem."

I lean my head against the glass window as Jeremiah drives. We mostly sit in silence as we pass through the city. Everything is beginning to look like it is moving slower. The cars mosey on by. The few people who are out in the street hang their heads low like zombies, walking inch by inch to their destination.

Jeremiah fiddles with the radio, trying to find a station. He opts for some country music that hums a quiet slow Southern tune.

I can't wait for all of this to be over. I can't wait to go to my father's house and tell him exactly what is causing this mayhem.

Hopefully it will be so terrifying and unnerving that it will snap him out of his trance and he'll immediately agree to head home with me to New Hampshire.

As I stare out the window, that's what I pray for. I wouldn't call myself religious, but I do believe in something. I have seen evil. In fact, I have been so close to evil that I have looked it square in the eye many times. That being said, my experience with *good* is quite lackluster. Oh how I would love to believe that there is some gracious benevolent God who wants nothing but good for the world.

Who believes that evil must be rooted out and that good should always prevail. I would love to believe that, but I just haven't seen it. I wouldn't say I am not religious. I just don't know to what extent. I do believe in something good. I have to or there would be no other reason worth living.

As we drive along the dreary road, I notice that Jeremiah has a little cross hanging around his rearview mirror that is held by a thin thread. It dangles as he drives down the winding roads closer and closer to the swamp. Along the edge of the road, the yellow mushrooms begin to get more dense and concentrated as we continue, like a little trail, leading us to more and more of the spores.

"What do you think is causing this?" I ask Jeremiah, breaking the silence.

Jeremiah shrugs his shoulders. "Heck if I know. That's why we brought you here, Ms. Brighton."

I nod. "Surely, you must have some sort of a guess if you already went out all this way? If you followed this trail, you must have some sort of hypothesis?"

Jeremiah shrugs and slows the truck down to a stop. He turns on the blinker and takes a right into the forest down a road that doesn't really look like a road at all. In fact, we are driving over rocks and boulders, and through a thick mud, running over hordes of spores as we descend into the swamp.

"Part of me thinks it's biblical," he says.

"Like, a plague?"

Jeremiah nods. He grips the wheel of the truck tighter as our ride begins to get rocky. Branches begin to hit the windshield as we dive deeper into the brush. Jeremiah turns on his windshield wipers, which flick off the mud, and the spores, that have been kicked up by the tires.

"God is mad, Beatrix. He's got a lot to be mad at in the world."

I shrug my shoulders as I stare out the window, watching the clusters of mushrooms get tighter and tighter. What starts as a dense line has formed into almost a wall of mushrooms by now. Some are as tall as my knees! One was so big it almost looked like a stool you could sit on.

"Just a bit further, Ms. Brighton. Once the road runs out, you'll know we made it."

As I look out the window, I finally see the first one. It's about the size of a small dog. A dead baby fawn lies on the ground, its body overwhelmed by spores. Growing out of its eyes, its mouth, and even its spine. I can't help but wonder if the spores caused its death.

"Now would be a good time to put on your mask, Ms. Brighton," Jeremiah says as he grips the wheel with one hand and puts his mask on with the other.

I nod and pull the mask over my face. It feels so foreign—like I am a warrior going into battle. The rubber seal presses against my skin, creating an uncomfortably tight grip around my face. Each breath comes with a mechanical wheeze through the filter cartridge. The straps dig into my scalp as I adjust them, trying to find the right balance between secure and suffocating.

The world looks different through the curved plastic eyepieces—slightly distorted at the edges, like I'm peering through a fishbowl. My peripheral vision is cut off by the mask's edges, forcing me to turn my head more to see around me. The inside of the mask quickly grows warm and humid with my breath.

I try to speak, but my voice comes out muffled and strange, like I'm talking underwater. My heart races a little faster—whether from restricted airflow or rising anxiety, I'm not sure. The weight of it reminds me that whatever we're heading into is real and dangerous. With each labored breath through the filter, I feel less like myself and more like some apocalyptic soldier.

I quickly realize that Jeremiah was right to have me put on my mask. As we descend further into the forest, the fog begins to thicken into a yellow mist so dense that we can barely see what is in front of us.

"We're almost there," Jeremiah says with a crooked tilt of his head.

The truck's headlights cut through the yellow mist like dull knives, barely illuminating a few feet ahead. Through my fogged mask, I can make out more shapes in the undergrowth—more dead animals, their bodies hosting colonies of those hideous mushrooms. A raccoon. A wild boar. Each corpse is a grotesque garden.

"There," Jeremiah says, pointing through the windshield.

The truck's beams catch something massive looming in the mist. At first, I think it's a hill, but as we draw closer, I realize it's a wall of fungus—yellow-orange caps larger than dinner plates climbing up the trunks of dead trees. The spores are so thick in the air here that they swirl in visible clouds, dancing in the headlight beams like toxic snow.

The mushrooms are so comically huge that I feel like we've driven into Wonderland.

Jeremiah kills the engine. The silence that follows feels heavy, oppressive. Even through the mask's filter, I can smell it now—a sickly sweet odor that reminds me of rotting fruit and wet earth.

"Welcome to ground zero, Ms. Brighton," Jeremiah says, his voice distorted through his mask. "Where it all started."

I clench my fists, my knuckles white. Whatever is causing this, whatever has my father in its grip—the answers are out there in that poisonous fog. And I'm going to have to walk right into it to find them.

CHAPTER 8

When I step out of Jeremiah's truck, my feet instantly sink into the ground and my gray running sneakers begin to soak. We've parked right in the middle of the swamp and the soft wet ground engulfs my feet. It's a thick mud and sludge that has been tainted a bright yellow.

"You shoulda worn boots," Jeremiah says as he walks around the truck.

I look down at my feet, which have almost disappeared into the dirt. "How am I supposed to walk through all of this?"

Jeremiah lets out a little laugh. "Pick up your feet, and walk quickly. Don't stand too long or you'll start to sink."

He puts his hand on my shoulder and points out into the distance. "You see that? That's where we're going."

It's hard to see because of the fog, but in the distance I can make out what looks to be a mushroom the size of Jeremiah's truck.

"We can't drive the truck out there," Jeremiah says. "The ground isn't stable. We'd get stuck. But we can walk. Should only take us twenty or so minutes."

I swallow hard. What have I gotten myself into? I'm no mycologist! I'm not even good at science. The last time I took a biology class was in undergrad almost twenty years ago. I can barely see a few feet in front of me! How am I supposed to determine what this is caused by?

The forest is eerily quiet as we stand looking into the distance. There's no sound of birds. No animals. Just the occasional breath of the spores. Each time they release a bit of gas into the air it sounds like they're coughing or letting out a little sigh. The bigger mushrooms are the loudest, letting out almost a rumble or a shake.

Are they watching us?

Can they hurt us?

As I look around the forest, I realize they are ubiquitous and we are just two little humans, surrounded by a highly complex, living and breathing network of toxic fungus.

"Well, you ready to get to steppin'?" Jeremiah says.

I shrug my shoulders. "Might as well." When I go to lift my feet, I feel a head rush like a wave running through my forehead. I feel woozy, and sick, and my knees begin to buckle.

Jeremiah quickly grabs me before I fall and helps me keep my footing.

"Easy there, Ms. Brighton," Jeremiah says.

"I'm sorry," I say as I struggle to gain my footing. "Head rush."

"It's easy to lose your mind out here. We have to keep moving. The more we stand still, the harder it gets to keep going."

"What do you mean?" I ask.

"I mean that if we dillydally too long in one spot, the fumes, they really start to eat away at you. Make you weak."

I nod and begin to trudge forward in the mud. "Well. Let's not waste any more time."

CHAPTER 9

"So—what are we looking for exactly?" Jeremiah asks as we trudge step by step into the depths of the swamp. We walk through a narrow lane, through mud that is flanked by mushrooms on each side. It almost looks like a road, perfectly cleared in the middle, leading us to the center of the chaos.

"Well," I say, taking a deep breath. It's hard to walk and talk at the same time. Our masks are working overtime to keep the toxic fumes out, but the air is still heavy. And it's hot. Oh so very hot. And the deeper we walk into the bayou, the hotter it gets. It's like we are making our way into a humid oven.

"If I could be honest, I am already inclined to think that something unnatural is causing this," I say.

Jeremiah turns to me. His bright eyes glow in the guard of his mask. "Why is that?"

I pause briefly and point at the two lines of mushrooms, lining our path. "Unnatural mushroom formation," I say out of breath. "Looks like it's manipulated by someone or something. Mushrooms don't grow in perfectly lined paths like some twisted yellow brick road."

Jeremiah nods and we keep walking.

"What else should we be looking out for?"

"Well, any unusual water patterns. Water flowing against the wind. Maybe animals exhibiting unusual behavior—although we may have that covered, really."

"Yeah, they're all dead," Jeremiah says. "I haven't seen one living thing in here besides us."

My stomach turns thinking about it. He's right. Not one living thing is in this swamp. Even the trees that should be flush with bright summer green leaves have turned into a decaying dark brown. Any animals that were in this swamp are already dead. My worries of getting bitten by a rogue alligator were assuaged when we passed several dead carcasses about a quarter of a mile ago.

"Any changes in air pressure, any weird markings, anything that looks like it could be an animal print but looks slightly . . . off."

Jeremiah nods. "What do they look like, the demons?"

I smile weakly. It's hard to explain these types of things to someone who has never seen them before.

"Well," I say. "Demons can look like everything and nothing at all. They can look like your best friend. They can look like a ghost. But in their true form, they're like . . . shadows that forgot how to behave. They move wrong, like watching someone walk through water but there's no water there. The edges of them aren't quite solid—they blur and shift, even when they're trying to hold a shape. And their eyes . . ." I pause, remembering. "Their eyes are always wrong. Even when they're pretending to be human, there's something about the eyes that makes your brain scream that something isn't right. It's like their eyes glow."

Jeremiah nods. "Well, Ms. Brighton. That sounds quite awful! What happens if we run into one of them demons out here?"

The hair on the back of my neck stands up. How did I not think of this earlier? Out here in the middle of a swamp, surrounded by gaseous spores—we'd be quite useless against a powerful demon! Then again, I'm usually never their target. For some reason, demons typically leave me alone. Maybe it's that I know too much or maybe I just don't fall for their tricks. But Jeremiah is different. He could be walking right into the path of a powerful and nasty demon.

Am I leading this kid like a poor little lamb to slaughter?

"Well, if we do run into one, you should run," I say. "You should run and you shouldn't worry about me. I can handle myself."

CHAPTER 10

I'm not sure how long we've been walking but it feels like hours and my brain is slowly becoming detached from my body. My legs are barely moving as we step through the thick mud, dodging rat carcasses, snakes, and rabbits. The giant mushroom in the distance only seems to get slightly closer as we walk.

I am sweating through my clothes.

"Do you know how much longer?" I ask.

Jeremiah hangs his head as he keeps trudging through the muck. "We will be there before you know it."

I sigh and continue to put one foot in front of the other, staring ahead as the towering mushroom seems to taunt me in the distance. With each step I feel my body getting more and more exhausted. My shirt is soaked with sweat and my feet are so completely drenched in swamp sludge that I've already forgotten my discomfort.

I'm doing this for my father.

I am here for my father.

I'm not sure if I am convincing myself or reminding myself at this point.

Not for some wild adventure. Not to save a city I barely know. I am here for truth and undeniable proof that something sinister is causing this outbreak of fungi.

And soon I will find it.

Just as I feel my body going numb, Jeremiah stops suddenly. "Did you feel that?" he asks, his voice oddly tight.

"Feel what?"

"The air . . . it just got cooler." He turns his head slowly, scanning the trees. "I think something's watching us."

He's right. The temperature has dropped dramatically, as if we've walked into a pocket of winter in the middle of the swamp. The air tastes different too—metallic, ancient.

That's when we see them through the trees—yellow lights dancing in the darkness, like fireflies grown too large. They pulse with an unnatural rhythm that makes my head swim, but I can't look away. They're beautiful, in a way that makes my chest ache with something like nostalgia.

"What is that?" I ask.

"We need to go that way," Jeremiah says, his voice taking on an odd, dreamy quality that matches the fog creeping into my thoughts.

The lights seem to dance just for us, beckoning with promises of answers. Each pulse sends waves of warmth through my tired body. How long have we been walking this path? The lights feel like rest, like truth, like everything we've been searching for.

"Trust me, Ms. Brighton. This is the right way."

But he's already moving toward the lights, climbing over the waist-high mushrooms with strange determination. I find myself following, drawn by that hypnotic glow. Each step toward the lights feels more right than the last.

"What about the big mushroom we were heading toward?" I hear myself ask, but the words feel distant, unimportant.

"This looks more promising. I think someone else is out here," Jeremiah calls back, voice muffled by the thickening air. "Come on. It's not that far."

I hesitate at the edge of the path, but the lights pulse again, and all my doubts melt away like frost in the morning sun. My feet seem to take on a life of their own, carrying me over the mushrooms and into the thicket. The spores around us dance in the strange light, and somewhere in the back of my mind, a voice whispers that I should be afraid.

But the lights are so beautiful, and we're so very, very close.

CHAPTER 11

Jeremiah leads me into the thicket as we continue off the path. The branches are thick and tangled, forcing us to duck and weave through the dense foliage. The yellow lights flicker through the branches, seeming to dance and beckon us forward. My clothes snag on thorns as we push deeper into the wilderness, the established path now completely lost behind us.

The air grows even colder, and I can see my breath forming clouds in front of my face. It doesn't make sense— it's the middle of summer in Louisiana. The temperature shouldn't be dropping like this. The mushrooms around us have changed too. Instead of the towering specimens we've been following, these are smaller, with caps that seem to glow with a faint bioluminescence in shades of pale green and blue.

I feel my brain getting slower with each step.

Everything begins to blur like it's happening in slow motion. Soon the breaths of the mushrooms are all that I can hear. In and out. In and out. The spores in this part of the woods look like they're emitting some type of steam. It's beautiful. A mist of glitter and gold seems to dance above them.

My mind feels cottony and light, like I'm floating just slightly above my own body. The spores swirl in hypnotic patterns. Some look like animals or even letters. Numbers. The yellow one looks like the number seven. And the blue one tastes like peppermint.

I can't tell anymore if the lights we're following are real or just fragments of my spore-addled imagination. Each breath draws more of the shimmering mist into my lungs, and the forest around me begins to pulse with an otherworldly glow.

"Ms. Brighton?" Jeremiah's voice sounds distant, as if he's calling to me from underwater. "Ms. Brighton—are you OK? You don't look so good."

But I can't focus on his words anymore. The mushrooms are singing to me now, their breath becoming a symphony that drowns out everything else. The world tilts and sways, golden spores dancing like stars falling from heaven. They're so beautiful. So perfect. I think I finally understand what they want to show me.

"I'm OK," I say as the words flow out of my body like diarrhea. I don't even have control of them, they are just leaking out of my body word by word. "We are almost there."

The lights in the distance get closer.

And closer.

Until I can see exactly what they are! And I am excited.

My head sways and swoons; it's like my head is rushing constantly with a never-ending high.

"Do you see it?" Jeremiah asks.

He walks up beside me and takes off his mask, holding it in his hand. It's like he can't believe his eyes. His jaw is open as he breathes in and out the glimmering shimmering mist.

I blink.

And blink again.

I can't believe what I'm seeing. Where the lights are coming from.

Up ahead of us there is a clearing, surrounded on all sides by a ring of large and lumpy spores. In the middle of the clearing is a brightly lit cottage—the lights we've been chasing.

Are we hallucinating?

Like Jeremiah, I slide off my mask to get a better look at the cottage.

Through the golden haze of spores, a structure materializes that makes my blood run cold. It's a cottage, but one that defies all natural law. Perched atop two massive chicken legs, each as thick as an ancient oak, the building sways ten feet above the swamp. The legs aren't just attached to the cottage—they're alive, their scaly surface rippling with muscle beneath a coating of yellow-tinged fungi. Massive talons, each longer than my arm, dig trenches in the earth as the entire structure shifts its weight from side to side.

The cottage itself is something from a nightmare— fence posts made of human bones ring its perimeter, skulls mounted on each one, weeping yellow spores from their eye sockets. The roof comes to a point so sharp it seems to tear at the sky, and from its eaves hang things that twist and writhe in the stagnant air.

I blink hard, willing the vision away. But with each blink, the cottage only becomes more real, more wrong. The legs twitch and flex, tendons visible through the fungal growth, and the whole building rocks like a predator preparing to pounce.

"Are those chicken legs?" My voice sounds distant, dreamlike. As if it's coming from someone else.

Jeremiah says nothing. His bloodshot eyes are fixed on the cottage, his face a mask of terrifying reverence.

The world begins to tilt. My head feels impossibly heavy, like it's being pulled toward the earth by invisible hands. The spores around us dance faster now, their movement making my vision swim. Windows like lidless eyes stare down at us, their warm light promising both welcome and doom.

"Oh God," I whisper, as centuries of folklore crystallize into horrible reality. "It's her. The Mother of Mushrooms."

The cottage looms larger with each passing second, though I can't tell if it's growing or if we're being drawn closer. Reality bends and warps around it like light through murky water. The legs stretch impossibly tall, and the whole structure seems to rear up against the yellow sky.

Colors melt and run together—the sickly glow from the windows, the golden clouds of spores, the bone-white fence posts—until the world becomes a carousel of nightmare images. Each rotation brings the cottage's true nature into sharper focus, each turn revealing some new horror I wish I could unsee.

Jeremiah's voice reaches me as if through layers of thick wool. "Ms. Brighton! Ms. Brighton, hold on!"

But I'm already falling. My consciousness splinters and scatters like spores in the wind. The cottage towers above me, a monument to things that should not be, its chicken legs coiled and ready to give chase.

The door creaks open, and a burst of yellow spores crashes over me like a tsunami. I try not to breathe, but they're everywhere—in my nose, my mouth, behind my eyes. Each spore feels alive, burrowing into my consciousness. My thoughts fragment and spiral. The world warps like a funhouse mirror, then snaps back. The last thing I remember is the taste of earth when my face hits the ground, and then my brain simply . . . stops.

Then nothing but the dark.

CHAPTER 12

When I wake up my neck is cramped and my head is tucked into my chest and my knees are pulled close to me. On the back of my neck I feel wooden bars pushing down, forcing me into the fetal position.

I am afraid to open my eyes but I can tell that I am trapped in a box or a cage. The cracks of a fire snap in the background. It's hot and I am drenched in sweat. The earthy smell of the spores stings my nostrils. I quietly feel around in my cage for my mask, but I feel nothing.

Should I open my eyes? Deep down, I know exactly what I am going to see. I've heard this story a thousand times. I just never thought I would be in it.

Almost a decade ago, I found myself in Minsk under rather unusual circumstances. This was 1987, and Americans didn't just casually visit the Soviet Union, especially not Byelorussia. But I had built something of a reputation in Eastern Europe for handling . . . unusual problems. The kind that official channels preferred to pretend didn't exist.

My invitation came through layers of bureaucracy, each more opaque than the last. First, a contact in the Romanian Ministry of Culture, then a series of letters through East German diplomatic channels, and finally official permission from Moscow itself. The problem, it seemed, was serious enough that ideology took a back seat.

I was brought to Ratomka, a village outside Minsk that housed one of the USSR's premier equestrian facilities. The center was their pride—training Olympic athletes and breeding some of the finest horses in the Eastern Bloc. But something was wrong. Horses were dying, and not in any way that made sense to their veterinarians or security personnel.

My official handler was from the Ministry of Sport, a serious man named Viktor who had clearly been chosen for his fluent English and Western manners. But it was obvious he reported to other, less *visible* authorities. They housed me in a guest wing of the facility director's residence—a surprisingly luxurious arrangement by Soviet standards, though I had no illusions about the rooms being bugged.

My translator was more interesting—an elderly woman named Irina Petrova. She'd spent five years in London during the 1950s as part of the Soviet trade mission, which explained her perfect English. But there was something in the way she looked at me when we discussed the incidents that suggested she knew more than she was saying.

"The horses," she told me that first night, her voice barely above a whisper, "they are not the first. There are stories in this village. Old stories. But no one speaks of them anymore."

We were sitting in what passed for my living room, a well-appointed space that would have been impressive anywhere in the USSR. Through the window, I could see the lights of the equestrian center, and beyond that, the dark line of the forest. The same forest where, according to the official reports, they'd found the first horse three months ago.

I'd handled cases in Romania, yes. Darker things that lurked in the Carpathian Mountains. But this felt different. In Romania, the authorities turned a blind eye to the old beliefs, letting people hang their crosses and garlic. Here in the heart of scientific socialism, even acknowledging something supernatural would be dangerous. Yet they'd called me anyway.

That should have been my first warning.

"What do you think is causing this?" I asked Irina one night as we sipped a cup of tea.

Irina shifted back and forth in her seat. "You know, I am happy I was tasked to help on this because I do believe."

"Believe in what?" I asked.

Irina whispered softly, and I was unsure if she was embarrassed to discuss the topic or wary that our room may be bugged. "I believe in demons. I've seen them. So when they asked me to come help you, I was just excited to finally meet someone who understands."

I nodded empathically. It was a story I heard a lot around the world. People were always happy to finally meet someone who understood.

"What did you see?" I asked her.

Irina folded her shaking leathery hands across her lap. "When I was a young girl, I was out walking in the woods with my brother. It was late at night and we should have been heading home, but we saw this light in the distance that was so intriguing we just had to follow it. Before we knew it we were lost in the woods."

Irina shifted in her seat and looked out the window that showed just a glimpse of the thick Belarusian forest.

"And then we saw her," Irina said as her voice cracked. "She was standing outside of this cottage that was walking on thick, crooked chicken legs with these long talons. She looked like an old woman at first, but when we looked closer, we could see her eyes glow."

"What was she?"

Tears welled in Irina's eyes. "She had this long nose that almost looked like a finger protruding from her face. And these pimply warts. And her teeth! Like jagged piano keys sprouting from her mouth in all different directions. I wanted to run, but my brother, he didn't. He was drawn to her like a moth to a flame. It was the last time I saw him."

"And she was a demon?" I asked.

Irina shrugged her shoulders and looked out the window. "A demon, I think. Others will say she's an old crone. That she doesn't exist, but I saw her that night. She's real. Her name is Baba Yaga."

CHAPTER 13

B aba Yaga. Mother of Mushrooms. As I'm sat curled up in the wooden cage, I can't bring myself to open my eyes. How could I be so foolish? So naive. To walk right into danger without my eyes wide open. I can't believe Jeremiah and I were foolish enough to walk right into her trap.

I have to open my eyes.

I have to confront this head-on.

In all of my time exploring demons and the paranormal, I've gotten myself into some pretty precarious situations—but this is by far the worst. I've never been so helpless. Cramped. Trapped. Sitting in a cage like livestock.

Baba Yaga's story was one I was quite familiar with—an old Russian crone who is typically depicted as baiting young children into her home and eating them. Most popular depictions show her wooden cottage with chicken feet and many call her a dryad or a wood nymph. Many call her a demon. In some other versions of folklore, she has been depicted as helping heroes, but given that I am trapped in a cage on the rusty floor of her walking cottage, I have a feeling that this Baba Yaga is not going to help me in the slightest.

Something shakes my cage violently, causing me to open my eyes.

"Ms. Brighton!" Jeremiah whispers.

I see Jeremiah standing over me with his watery, bloodshot eyes. He's teary-eyed. I look around the cottage, which is small and rustic. There's one other cage in the corner with a young girl sitting in it with her knees tucked to her chest. She looks no more than nine or ten and has bright blond hair. She's rocking back and forth, staring into the distance.

"Miss Brighton, I'm awful sorry," Jeremiah says, his fingers trembling against my cage. "Lord, I'm so sorry. Was fixin' to bring your daddy out here instead. He's just an old man. Didn't reckon anybody'd miss him much, but he couldn't make it this far out in the swamp—I—"

The words hit me in my gut.

"You brought me here?" I say as my voice shakes.

I look around the room and there is no sign of the old crone. Just a big crackling fire in the middle of the room with a large cauldron hanging from the ceiling, swaying slowly over the flames.

I try to maneuver my body so I can look up at Jeremiah but my cage is just too small.

"Jeremiah, get me out of here!" I say.

Jeremiah lowers down and brings his finger up to his mouth to shush me. "Miss Brighton, hush now." Jeremiah's voice drops to a hoarse whisper. "She's comin'."

I grab the wooden rails of the cage and shake them so hard my knuckles turn white. "Get me out! Get me out now!"

"Miss Brighton, you gotta understand." Jeremiah's voice cracks. "If I didn't bring her somebody else, she was gonna take my baby sister. She was gonna take my Jenny," he says, pointing to the little girl huddled in the corner.

"What do you mean?" My head spins. I just can't believe this. I knew Jeremiah was a bit off—but I never thought he would betray me!

"She was in my truck when I came out here to explore what was happening with the spores. She was supposed to stay put but before I knew it, she followed me out into the swamp and that's when I saw her."

"Baba Yaga?"

"Shhh . . . she will hear you!" Jeremiah says as his face turns white. "She did this. She did all of this. *She's* the Mother of Mushrooms."

I swallow hard and lay my head against the wooden rail. "So after all of this you're just going to leave me here? To die?"

Jeremiah swallows hard and looks away from me.

"You were never here to help my father. He trusted you with every ounce of his soul. And you just wanted a replacement for your sister?" I look up at the girl in the corner whose face is white and frail. Her hair is scruffed and greasy and her eyes look creamy and pink.

"She's been here over a week," Jeremiah says. "I don't even think she's eaten. She won't even talk to me!"

He turns to his sister and whispers. "Jenny! Please, say something."

The little girl looks at her brother and says nothing. Her eyes are empty, like she can barely hear what he's saying. Unlike me, she fits a bit better in the cage and far less cramped but she's surrounded by a ring of mushrooms that are puffing yellow mist all around her. After a week of this, she's probably completely delusional.

"She can't stay out here with *her*. I think she's going to hurt her. She's going to do something horrible, I just know it," Jeremiah whispers.

"She eats children!" I say as I shake my cage. "And she's going to eat me too if you don't get me the fuck out of here. Just let us both out, Jeremiah. We can all leave."

He shakes his head. "We'll never make it. Not through the forest. We'll pass out. Be delusional. It's like Dorothy walking through the poppies. We'll collapse and fall asleep and she'll just get all of us then. I didn't come all this way to die too."

"Jeremiah, we have the masks. We can carry your sister and make a run for it. Come on, don't do this. Don't give one life for another. Please just let me out!"

Jeremiah looks down at the cage and looks over to his sister. By the tears in his eyes I can tell he is thinking twice about bringing me here. He's not evil. He's just desperate. I would be too if it was my little sister.

His lip trembles as if he is about to burst into tears.

As much as I want to blame him, kill him even, I can't. If it was my father in that cage, I would do anything to get him out.

"Come on, Jeremiah," I say. "Don't do this. The same way that you have to save your sister, I have to save my father. And I can't do that if I am stuck in this cage. Please let me out. We can get out of here together. We can fix this together. Let's go after the old witch. There are three of us and one of her. We can end this."

"We can?" Jeremiah asks. He takes the sleeve of his shirt and wipes away some yellow milky tears.

"Yes, I promise. We can do this. I've been in worse, much scarier situations." That is a lie of course, but I can't help myself. This is about survival. "So all you need to do is get one of those knives hanging up on the wall over there and cut the ties on this cage. And let me out. And we can get out of here and get you and your sister home safely."

Jeremiah looks down at me and clenches his fists so hard that his knuckles turn white. He looks to the long, dull, rusty knives that are hanging in a jumbled mess of cooking ware next to Baba Yaga's cauldron.

"OK. I'll do it."

CHAPTER 14

I sit in the cage and watch as Jeremiah walks toward the knives hanging in the front. I watch as his body shakes with each step on the dirty wooden floor. The floor groans as he steps on the floorboards and he walks cautiously, afraid to make a sound.

I can't help but wonder what he's so afraid of.

Baba Yaga is an old woman. A witch. A crone!

Surely the three of us could take her if we tried.

I sit in my cage anxiously as I grip the bars, hoping that Jeremiah will hurry up and make all of this end before she gets here.

Just as Jeremiah reaches for the knife dangling in the air next to the witch's other pots and pans, the house suddenly lurches violently to the left. As if the chicken decided to stand on one leg instead of the other.

I grip the bars of the cage tightly as my wooden box slides across the room to the same corner as Jenny.

The shaking causes Jeremiah to fall to the ground and just as he struggles to regain his footing, the cottage lurches again to the other side.

"She's coming!" Jeremiah yells as he scrambles.

My breath sits in the back of my throat mixed with the vomit that I feel rising from my stomach. I feel so paralyzed by fear. In reality I want to slap myself for being so goddamn embarrassing. I'm a demonologist! Not some helpless little lamb stuck in a cage.

"She's going to be here any minute," Jeremiah says as he stands upright.

The house stops shaking as Jeremiah walks into the corner by the door. He's crying and shaking and he doesn't have the knife.

"Jeremiah—get the fucking knife!" I yell. "Get it now!"

He shakes his head as he folds his arms across his chest and closes his eyes. "I can't, Miss Brighton. I can't. I can't risk her taking my Jenny!"

I open my mouth to speak—to cuss this fool out who has gotten us into such a terrible mess, but footsteps interrupt me. Loud and heavy they get closer and closer to the door as Jeremiah continues to cower, afraid of the crone.

As the witch gets closer I close my eyes and try to remember everything that I can about Baba Yaga. When you're dealing with an entity like this—knowledge is power.

About ten years ago I wrote a book called *The Complete Guide to Demons and Demonology*. It was a very thorough and long project that took me years to put together and discusses just about every demon you've ever heard of under the sun. Baal, imps, Lilith, succubi—and there was one very small part about Baba Yaga that reads:

Baba Yaga: The Mother of Mushrooms, A Parasitic Entity

63

While most demons manifest through fire and brimstone, Baba Yaga spreads her influence through decay and fungal growth. My research in Eastern Europe, particularly in Belarus and Western Russia, suggests she is neither purely demon nor faery, but something that exists in the spaces between classification.

Her most recognizable feature, according to eyewitness accounts from the Minsk region, is her mobile dwelling—a cottage that walks on massive chicken legs. Witnesses describe the structure as being alive, with the legs actively hunting like a predator stalking prey. The cottage is said to be perpetually surrounded by mushrooms and fungal growth, though accounts vary on their exact nature.

Signs of infestation include but are not limited to:

- Unusual fungal growths that resist normal removal methods
- Unexplained disappearances, particularly of children
- Strange lights in wooded areas
- Metallic taste in the air
- Unusual wildlife behavior

What makes Baba Yaga unique among demonic entities is her binding to an ancient truth-telling pact. According to manuscripts I discovered in Romania's Carpathian archives, she must answer three questions truthfully when properly addressed. The exact phrasing, passed down through generations of Eastern European demonologists, is:

"Grandmother of the Forest, Bearer of Ancient Wisdom, I seek three truths from your lips."

This compulsion to truth-telling represents her only known vulnerability, though I have yet to document a successful implementation of this method. The challenge lies not just in the asking, but in surviving long enough to complete all three questions. The few recorded attempts suggest that the questions must be precisely worded, as Baba Yaga is notorious for twisting imprecise language to her advantage.

Baba Yaga can be defeated by seeking truth from her lips. But very few have lived to tell the tale.

CHAPTER 15

I smell her before I see her.

It's a rotten and putrid smell with a hint of manure that floods the cottage before she even walks through the door. We hear her outside breathing heavily as if she's about to run out of air. Each booming step is paired with a breathy gasp as if she is going to blow down the house.

The cottage lurches violently as she rips open the door with her long fungus-filled talons.

When I turn to see her my heart skips a beat.

I'm not staring at an old woman—or even a crone for that matter. I'm staring at something evil. She's more of a creature than a woman. A cryptid, even.

Baba Yaga doesn't walk into the room—she hobbles into it, with big booming steps. Moss fills her silver and scraggly hair, draping down her face like seaweed. Her teeth are long and jagged like broken piano keys jutting out at impossible angles, some yellowed ivory, others blackened with rot, all of them moving independently like fingers seeking prey. Yellow mushrooms sprout from between them, their caps glistening with moisture as they pulse in time with her belabored breathing.

Her skin isn't skin at all—it's a living carpet of yellowy moss with bright yellow spores protruding from her neck and shoulders like cancerous growths. Where her fingers should be, long yellow talons twist and writhe, their nails splitting with yellow fungus.

The temperature rises as she enters and the air gets so heavy it feels like oxygen is being sucked out of the room. I feel her heat radiating across the space between us—damp and drenched with decay. A cluster of mushrooms suddenly bursts from her cheek, spreading open like a blooming flower to reveal a second mouth underneath; this one full of thin needlelike teeth that chitter and click together like it's speaking in tongues.

This is the Mother of Mushrooms.

I want to scream—but I know I am the only one who can save us. I am our only chance. Our last hope.

Jeremiah still stands in the corner weeping and whimpering like a puppy. Baba Yaga looks at him and offers a crooked smile.

"You've brought me a fresh one I see!" she says. She narrows her eyes and looks down at me in the cage as she hobbles closer. The mushrooms on her body begin to puff a yellow mist. She pauses when she gets a good look and a frown erupts over her face.

"I asked for a child! And you brought me an old woman."

I've never been called an old woman in my life, but if it keeps me alive, I will gladly take it.

She spins on her cracked heels toward Jeremiah, spitting and spewing in fury. "This isn't what I want! I don't want her!"

"Then let me go!" I yell.

She spins back around on her heels and I see her eyes gleam a bright yellow. "In this house you do not speak unless you are spoken to. Do you understand me?"

I bite my lip. I have to say it. I have to outsmart her.

My voice comes out as a whisper. Every instinct is telling me to run but I am trapped in this cage with nowhere to go. "Mother of Mushrooms, I seek three truths from your lips."

Her frown fades as her whole body convulses, mushrooms erupt and wither across her form in waves. Her eyes widen until they take up almost half of her face. She can't help herself.

She has to answer.

And she has to tell the truth.

The truth is the only thing that will set us free.

The sound that comes from both her mouths is like wet meat slapping against stone.

"Three truths? You want three truths? I'll give you three truths" Her voice resonates from every fungal growth, a chorus of wet whispers. A large mushroom cap splits open on her forehead, revealing a third eye that weeps yellow fluid.

She leans in closer and smells me, taking in a big whiff of air.

"On second thought. She will do. She smells so sweet. So . . . delectable. A sweet morsel."

The creature is drooling now, a thick yellow oil that drips down her mouth and onto the floor next to me. I can see my reflection in the little pools.

"My tender little breakfast. Ask your questions, then. Let me savor your desperation."

I swallow hard, mustering every last ounce of courage I have. "Mother of Mushrooms, what gives life to your spores?"

The crone lets out a low growl. "Like calls to like, precious one." Her breath hits my face, smelling of rot and copper. "My children dance where I dance, feast where I feast, sleep where I sleep." Her fungal fingers reach down to touch my cheek through the wooden bars, leaving tiny spores that begin to sprout instantly against my skin. I frantically wipe them away as she continues, "They are my footprints, nothing more. Every home needs its garden, after all."

I'm so terrified I can barely think, but I force my mind to work. Focus. Analyze. Stay alive. "How do your spores spread?"

Baba Yaga begins to walk around my cage, sizing me up like her next meal.

"What creature doesn't seek warmth?" Her voice rings in my ear like an earworm. "What child doesn't return to its mother's hearth?" Something wet drips onto my shoulder—I look down to see yellow ichor eating through my shirt, tiny mushrooms already beginning to form in the holes. "My little ones only wish to come home, to return to where they first drew breath." Her fungal talons touch my hair through the top of the cage, leaving spores that make my scalp crawl.

"They remember where they were born, you see. They always remember their first home."

My mind races even as my body trembles with fear. The first two answers—I have to decode them quickly before I waste my final question. She keeps referring to "home" and "hearth," making the cottage central to everything. Like calls to like. *Children returning to mother's hearth.* The mushrooms aren't just spreading randomly—they're extensions of her. They're her children and they all lead back here. But why? In all my years studying demons, the most powerful ones always have an anchor in our world. Something that lets them manifest physically.

My eyes dart around the cottage, taking in the wooden walls, the way every mushroom seems to orient toward her like flowers tracking the sun. Even the spores seem to spiral back to this point, this place.

And then it hits me—demons don't typically have physical forms unless . . . unless they're bound to something. The third question can't be about the mushrooms or the spread—it has to be about what binds her here.

What allows her to manifest. If I'm wrong about this, if I waste this last question . . . I try not to think about the consequences as I force my terror-frozen lips to form the words.

"What binds you to this realm?"

She moves in front of me again, her wretched body expanding, stretching as if she and her children are about to swallow me whole.

Her face splits open like a fungal bloom, those piano key teeth spreading out in a spiral pattern as she answers in a chorus of voices. "I am bound as any mother is bound—by the walls that shelter my children, by the roof that guards their sleep, by the hearth that warms their birth." Multiple mouths form and dissolve across her body as she speaks, each filled with those horrible ivory teeth.

"Cut a tree from its roots, and what becomes of its branches? Scatter the coals of a fire, and what becomes of its warmth?"

The cottage, I think.

The cottage isn't just her home, it's her body, her anchor to our realm. It all comes back to the cottage.

Destroy her home, destroy her.

But as her twisted form contorts with delight, as yellow spores rain down like toxic snow, as mushrooms begin sprouting from every surface of the cottage, I realize why she's so confident. We're trapped in here with her. Even if I've solved her riddle, what chance do I have of surviving long enough to use that knowledge?

My eyes dart to the cauldron hanging over her fire.

Unless . . .

The fire.

We have to burn the house.

We have to burn it all down.

CHAPTER 16

Baba Yaga towers over me, sizing me up like a snack. "Oh how my little meal thinks she's so smart. She will never get out of her cage until I let her out. How do you prefer to be prepared?" She cackles as she hobbles around my cage as the mushrooms on her writhe. "Sous vide? Roasted over the open fire? Grilled? I could be in the mood for a nice broil. You are my guest after all; however you prefer to be prepared I can accommodate."

I swallow hard.

I have to get her out of the cottage.

I have to burn it all down.

"Do you have a garden?" I ask as my voice trembles.

Baba Yaga pauses and nods. "I have one of the best gardens in the world."

"Well," I say, trying to buy myself just a little time. "I would like to be prepared with fresh herbs from your garden. Only the freshest."

Baba Yaga pauses and reaches one of her long wrinkly arms over her back and rips off a cluster of moss and mushrooms. "Truffles?"

"No. Herbs."

Baba Yaga nods. "Do you have a preference? I could go pick some thyme, or dill. Ooh. I find that rosemary goes very well with flesh with a little sea salt."

"That sounds great," I say. "If you're going to eat me, I prefer to be properly and heavily seasoned."

Baba Yaga nods. "Very well then. I will be out to the garden and back in a few." She hobbles over to Jeremiah who is still in the corner of the room whimpering and shaking. She walks up to him and touches one of her long talons to his cheek and a ray of spores instantly sprouts. Jeremiah's eyes widen as he looks down at the little colony sprouting on his skin.

"And if I see any of you try to pull any tomfoolery I am going to put all three of you in the same stew. Properly seasoned of course."

Baba Yaga turns away from Jeremiah and hobbles out the door of the cottage, leaving a trail of mushrooms in her place.

I wait to speak until I hear Baba Yaga walk away from the door. When I am sure that she's gone, I whisper to Jeremiah. "Jeremiah. I am going to save us. I promise—but you need to get me out of this cage."

Jeremiah shakes his head. "No. I can't let her hurt Jenny."

I grip the bars of the cage so tight my knuckles are white. "Jeremiah, I swear to God. On everything. If you get me out of this goddamn cage I can get us out of here! Please. Please. Just get the knife and cut me out."

"How do I know you're telling the truth? What if you escape on your own and just leave me here?"

"I would never do that, Jeremiah. I would never let her hurt you. I know how to destroy her and how to save Baton Rouge."

Jeremiah's eyes light up with a glimmer of hope. "Really?"

"Yes. Not only can I save us, but I can stop this. Once and for all. I just need you to get me out and I will handle the rest."

As Jeremiah walks across the room, he is shaking so much that he can barely keep his balance. I don't want to startle him—but he has to move quicker.

"Come on, Jeremiah, you can do this," I whisper as he delicately walks across the floor. "Do it for Jenny."

After what feels like an eternity, Jeremiah grabs the knife and walks his way over to my cage. He cuts the twine that holds the wooden cage together, tie by tie until the lid of the cage is undone and I can easily press out of the top.

I can finally stand! After what feels like being cramped in the tiny box for days. Hours. Minutes? Who knows how long we've been trapped in the cottage by now.

"Quick, go get Jenny," I say as I quickly begin to scramble around Baba Yaga's rustic kitchen. I know what I'm looking for—but I can't find it. The crone has jars upon jars of bizarre ingredients: crow's feet, lizard tongues, bat wings, pig fetus— and then I see it. I grab the big bottle and begin to walk toward the fire in the center of the room.

"Jenny!" Jeremiah yells as he lifts his little sister out of the cage. She looks like she can't hear him. She doesn't even react to the sound of his voice. Instead, she lies almost limp in his arms, staring into the distance. "We have to get her out of here. She's sick."

"We've got this," I say. "Now—I need you guys to hide by the door, and when she walks through it, you need to run out as quickly as possible."

"What about you?" Jeremiah asks.

"Don't worry about me. You need to get your sister to safety. Come back for me later if you can—but I will be alright."

I take the bottle of oil and begin to form a ring around the room, working to cover the entire cottage while creating a big pattern over the mushrooms that will hopefully cause Baba Yaga's little rustic cottage to burst into flames once I connect the ring back to the fire.

Jeremiah takes his place behind the door with his sister in his arms.

We are going to do this. We are going to break free.

CHAPTER 17

I'm only halfway through pouring the oil circle when the cottage lurches violently. The floorboards beneath us creak like breaking bones. The door bursts open so quickly with a gush of wind that it almost hits Jeremiah in the face.

"Oh, how adorable." Baba Yaga's voice drips with amusement as she hobbles into the building. "The little demonologist thinks she can play with fire."

My stomach drops. She knows.

"What, dearie? You don't think I know? You don't think I know that you're here to destroy me?" Her laugh sounds like crackling fungus. "Didn't your father teach you better? No, wait—he's too busy cultivating my garden in his brain."

Baba Yaga stands in the doorway, but something's different about her now. The mushrooms on her skin are splitting open, revealing wet, pulsing flesh underneath.

"You know what I love about scholars?" she muses, tilting her head at an impossible angle. "They always think knowledge will save them. But tell me, dear—what good are books when my children are growing?"

The floorboards rupture with a wet, meaty sound. Yellow tendrils thick as arms shoot up, but these aren't like the mushrooms outside. These are bigger. Slimier. Stronger. They wrap around my ankles, and I feel them pulsing against my skin—not like a heartbeat, but like thousands of tiny mouths opening and closing. One bites me. It stings as it crawls up my legs, sucking on my calves like tentacles.

"Can you feel them tasting you?" Baba Yaga purrs as the growths crawl higher. "They're so curious about your flavor. Unseasoned."

I try to scream but can't. The tendrils are at my knees now, and I can feel them trying to burrow through my flesh. Each point of contact burns like acid, and where they touch, my skin begins to transform. Little yellow caps push through my epidermis, stretching it until it splits.

Jeremiah makes a horrible choking sound. A mushroom has forced its way between his lips, its cap unfurling inside his mouth like a blooming flower. He drops Jenny on the ground and she falls with a hard thud. More sprout from his cheeks, stretching his skin until his face looks like a grotesque garden. Through it all, his eyes remain terrifyingly aware.

"Don't fight it," Baba Yaga coos, running a talon along my cheek. Where she touches, flesh becomes fungus. "Soon you'll be part of my family. Well, part of my children's dinner, but it's almost the same thing."

The tendrils reach my waist, dissolving fabric and burrowing into flesh. I feel them inside me now, spreading through my muscles like roots through soil. One brushes against my tongue and the taste—oh God, the taste. Like death and decay and sweet rot all at once.

"That's right," Baba Yaga whispers, noticing my expression. "They make everything better. Just ask your father. Ask everyone in Baton Rouge. Soon they'll all be in my garden."

The bottle feels impossibly heavy as mushrooms crawl up my arms. They're trying to pry my fingers open, to make me drop it.

"Still holding on to hope?" Baba Yaga clicks her teeth in disapproval. "Humans. Always thinking they can burn away their problems. But fire?" Her face splits into multiple grins. "Fire just spreads spores, little scholar. Or did you not read that chapter?"

I force her voice out of my brain.

She's wrong.

Destroy the cottage. Destroy Baba Yaga.

As mushrooms crawl up my throat I realize now is my only chance.

With every last bit of my strength, I hurl the bottle at the fire. Time seems to stop as I pray to God, Buddha, whoever, that the bottle hits at just the right angle to put an end to this horrible misery. Through mushroom-clouded eyes, I see Baba Yaga's expression shift from amusement to anxiety.

"Clever girl," she whispers. "You won't—"

The bottle shatters. For a moment, nothing happens. Then we are consumed by light. Screaming. Yelling.

I feel the tentacles release me like an octopus running back to hide under a rock, but the room is surrounded by flames. Baba Yaga's body ignites like a torch, her mushroom flesh sloughing away in burning sheets as she reaches for me with blazing hands.

The door is open.

Jeremiah is picking up Jenny to carry her out.

Flames rise as high as my head as I am surrounded by scorching heat on all sides.

As Baba Yaga begins to burn, she watches me with her big bright yellow eyes. She reaches out her hand to grab me but I back up, falling into the flame that burns my skin.

I have to get out of here. Now.

There's so much fire between me and the door. So much fire. Exactly how I designed it.

I close my eyes, and pray, and run into the flames as fast as I can.

CHAPTER 18

When I open my eyes I see the bright clear sky and everything burns. My legs, my hands—everything feels raw. My head pounds like the worst migraine that I have ever had. I try to sit up—but I can't. I am too exhausted. So tired that I could fall back asleep.

"You're awake!"

A little girl stands over me with bright blond hair. She smiles from ear to ear like it's the best news she's heard all day. Her eyes are a bright topaz that shine in the daylight. As her grin widens, I notice something odd about her teeth—they're too uniform, too straight, almost like little white piano keys lined up in perfect rows.

It takes me a minute—but I recognize her. It's Jenny. She's got a bit of ash all over her face but she no longer looks like she's drained. In fact, she looks bright and bubbly.

"Miah! Come here, she's awake!"

Jeremiah appears standing over me. He looks like hell—but his eyes are no longer bloodshot and jaundiced. His hand absently rubs at his chest, fingers tracing patterns where I swear I saw mushrooms bursting through his skin.

"Where am I?" I ask. I need water. ASAP. My mouth is dry like I swallowed the desert whole. I run my fingers through my hair and they come away dusted with fine yellow powder. I try to brush it off my clothes but it clings like it's rooted there.

"Been carryin' you," Jeremiah says, breathing heavily. "Almost back to the truck now. Just a little ways more. Had to rest myself a bit. We wandered way off into the deep swamp."

I take a deep breath and taste the air. It's lighter. It's still Baton Rouge in the summer but . . . I can see the sun! It shines right behind Jeremiah's head, hanging in the sky that looks clear as day.

"Did we do it?" I ask. "Did we destroy the cottage?"

Jeremiah looks down at me and narrows his eyes, his hand still absently rubbing his chest. "Cottage?"

"Yes!" I say. "Baba Yaga's cottage."

He shakes his head as if he can't remember.

Is this a joke?

Am I hallucinating?

"She tried to kill us! And eat us! And we had to burn down the cottage to save Baton Rouge—and that's how I got all of these burns!" Furious, I will myself up and point at my legs . . . which are . . . totally fine. A little scruffed up sure, but definitely not burned.

Jeremiah lets out a low laugh. "Heck, Ms. Brighton. I don't know anything about a cottage or a Baba Yaga. All I know is that you and I fell asleep out here in these mushroom fields some time ago. We must've been knocked out for a day or two. Thank God Jenny and my Pops were able to come out here and get us."

"Your Pops?" I frown as Jeremiah points behind me.

I turn around and see an older gentleman in a bright orange hunting jacket.

"Cops wouldn't come out this way 'cause of all of the mushrooms but about a day ago they all disappeared. Turned to dust they did," explained Jeremiah's father. "Sun came back out. When I hadn't heard from Jeremiah in a few days thought I'd go out looking for him. I knew he'd be in this swamp. He wanted to get down to what was happening so badly. Found you two passed out."

Jenny skips over to me, that too-perfect smile still plastered on her face. "Everything's better now," she says, and for a moment her teeth seem to shift and realign, like keys on a piano being played. "The mushrooms are gone. They're all gone." But as she speaks, I notice yellow spores falling from her hair like gentle snow.

CHAPTER 19

The late summer air in New Hampshire feels clean in my lungs. It's been two weeks since I left Baton Rouge, and I still find myself checking the corners of rooms for yellow growths, still catch myself holding my breath when I open doors.

My father calls every morning now. Not just the occasional check-in, but real conversations. Today, I'm sitting on my front porch with a cup of coffee when the phone rings.

"The sun is so bright today," he says instead of hello. "I forgot how beautiful it could be."

"Dad, please," I try one last time. "Come stay with me. Just for a while. Who knows if it could come back. I don't feel safe with you being there and staying put. What if there are long-term effects? What if your house has black mold or worse!"

He laughs, but it's gentle. "Beatrix, for the first time in months, I can think clearly. And what I'm thinking is that I love this house, whatever happened here—and I know something happened, even if my memory of it feels like a dream."

"It was worse than that, Dad," I remind him. "It was evil. Pure evil."

"I know," my father says. "And you saved us all. Even if Jeremiah doesn't remember. Even if he thinks it's crazy, I believe you, Bea. There's no other way that it all suddenly disappears—unless you fixed it. I knew you could do it. I believe you now," he says, his voice earnest. "About everything. The demons, the ghosts, all of it. I should have believed you when you were my little girl crying to me about a ghost in the barn. I should have listened to you. And I'm sorry I didn't. It will haunt me every day."

I feel tears welling up. After all these years of sideways looks and awkward silences whenever I mentioned my work, hearing those words means more than I can say.

"The university's even offering me tenure," he continues. "Can you believe it? They say my research the past few months has been groundbreaking. Even if I can't quite remember doing it."

"Dad . . ."

"I know you're worried. But I've never felt more clear-minded. More alive. Whatever was here, you drove it out. You did that."

After we hang up, I sit on the porch drinking my coffee, watching the sun play through the autumn leaves. Maybe he's right. Maybe everything really is fine now.

That's when I see it.

There, between the weathered boards of my porch steps, a spot of yellow. Just one tiny mushroom, no bigger than my thumbnail. Its cap glistens with morning dew, and as I stare at it, I swear I can hear it breathing.

I reach down to pluck it, but stop. What if it multiplies?

The mushroom seems to sway back and forth, as if it recognizes me. Like it's waving to me.

Evil doesn't die. It just finds new places to grow.

EV Dean brings haunting New England folklore to life from the shadows of Los Angeles. A Phillips Exeter alum whose horror fiction walks the knife-edge between reality and nightmare, Dean has cultivated a devoted following with her chilling Bunny Foo Foo series and the acclaimed Darkest Hour novellas. **You can follow EV Dean on Instagram at @ EVDean_author or visit their website at EVDeanWrites. com.**

www.ingramcontent.com/pod-product-compliance
Lightning Source LLC
Chambersburg PA
CBHW051932240626
47153CB00004B/1461